Raftery's Ghost

·······························

A Mac and Millie Mystery

JB Michaels

Harrison and James Publishing

Contents

To the Raftery Family

To Mike and Marcia, thanks for the encourage-
ment and support.

Author's Note

Upon meeting my mother-in-law in the summer of 2012, she talked about Geneva Illinois with much love and affection, and the very first attraction she spoke of was The Little Traveler. The incredible retail mansion with 36 rooms. She'd asked if I had visited the Traveler and I said yes, a long time ago on a short daytime visit to Geneva after my mom and sisters shopped the picturesque and popular Third Street. At that point, I had maintained only a vague remembrance. Her enthusiasm and my curiosity urged me to visit the Traveler as soon as possible.

Since that initial conversation, I have visited the Traveler many times, shopped there, walked around, ate at the Atrium Café, and of course signed books there. For most of my life, I noted my three favorite places: my Grandparent's house, Wrigley Field, and Walt Disney World. There is a fourth favorite place now: The Little Traveler. It has brought my family and I much joy and of course sparked my very active imagination.

To give a bit of context, I grew up watching classic films like 'The Thin Man' series, Agatha Christie adaptations, Charlie Chan, Basil Rathbone's Sherlock Holmes, and many other murder mystery films such as the cult classic 'Clue'. My grandparents nurtured a love for 1930s Golden Age of Hollywood in me and walking the Traveler's rooms inspired me to write 'Raftery's Ghost'. The rich history of The Little Traveler combined with the suspense of a murder mystery set in the historic building's storied walls seemed a winning combination.

If you are a fan of or have read my work, you will notice I don't spend paragraphs on superfluous detail, I like to get to the point. I like to paint enough of a picture and then let the reader's imagination fill the rest in. 'Raftery's Ghost' could easily translate to other forms of storytelling. The book's setting and plot could be a stage play, as it takes place in our beloved Tiny Wanderer on one dark and stormy night...

RAFTERY'S GHOST

By JB Michaels

One

--- -- -------------------------------

My initial reluctance to take on this peculiar case is one borne of fear. There, I admit it. I so foolishly and humbly lay my lack of courage at the feet of the protracted disappearance of one aristocratic daughter of England: Lady Raftery, who ventured to America with nary a doubt in her mind that she would face any adversity as someone of her birthright would tend to think-- or not think, in this circumstance. Despite her mother's constant nagging and shoving of pamphlets reporting young women's disappearances upon arrival in American cities;

these young women, if found, were forced into sex slavery. All manner of awful detail notwithstanding, I did not want to examine more closely this dark side of American urban life.

Please do take this all with a grain of salt, for I wouldn't be relaying these notes if I hadn't taken it on. I certainly did take it on. The sum of British pounds heaped onto my desk in my office on Baker Street did much to convince me and push down any sort of nausea associated with what I could find myself investigating. I welcomed an all-expenses-paid trip to America. The Great War is a few years past and times are good in the ole US of A, well, for the most part. I don't understand why they prohibited alcohol. This is exactly why we British were happy when those religious zealots left. Religion had been far too prominent in their lives and now their legacy of strictness has led them to ban spirits. Of course, most people find ways to drink no matter the law of the land. With my time here, there are many places to drink and gamble and be merry. It's almost as if the law has given way to an even wider, more accepted debauchery.

That which is prohibited is that much more desirable.

I did run into some rough gentlemen during my investigations in Chicago. Silk suits, quite oily hair, fedoras. Perhaps 'gentlemen' is too kind of a word for these fellows. Thuggery seems a more appropriate adjective. A rogue's gallery, as it were. One gentleman, ahem sorry thug, who held much power in the speakeasy I found myself in, had a nasty scar across his cheek. A symbol synonymous with societal menace and power. I finished my brandy and left that joint with my bones intact, thankfully.

I held a picture of Lady Raftery everywhere I went. I surveilled the city and marched up and down the streets. I, at last, contacted a distant cousin of Lady Raftery who arrived from a three-week trip to the Orient, and she relayed that the Lady left Chicago and ventured to a small town west of the city called Geneva. My mind immediately flashed of Viking helmets and marauders pillaging abbeys of my dear England. I tend to romanticize everything. My mind wanders often, which is surprising since I am so good at my occupation. Anyway, I digress. Why Lady Raftery would leave the bustling, lively metropolis for a small village is beyond me. Perhaps she tired of the crowds, debauchery, and smell of Chicago. She likely sought the familiar, a more palatial parity, as that of her native English countryside where she matured.

Why wouldn't she wire her family of her locale? This was the mystery that kept me sleuthing, as it were.

I arrived in Geneva and have set myself to the task of finding her which should, by all logic, prove much easier given Geneva's size in contrast to Chicago. The people of Geneva pointed me to a shop of antiquity called The Tiny Wanderer, which is where I now write this summary. People say that she comes in here periodically. It is an American mansion, I suppose. A big home that has been converted into a shop of interesting items that span the world. It is the talk of the town and a place of interest for shoppers and curious people everywhere. Japanese swords, dresses, Chinese finger traps, jade statues, even ancient middle eastern tablets. All for sale! It is no doubt capitalizing on the recent fascination with archeology stemming from the discovery of Tut's tomb.

The same ghostly nonsense of Tut's tomb infected and enraptured the imagination of the locals in Geneva. I have been here only a day and a half and have heard the haunting tales of The Tiny Wanderer. That the items inside this estate hold unearthly power, even spirits, from beyond. The most ridiculous element of this nonsense is that the very staff of The Tiny Wanderer are the ones spreading these tales of terror. Tales that include people entering the store and never exiting. That certain souls are forever trapped in the walls of this house.

I finished my tea and took a stroll. My hand is still trembling a bit as I have come back to record what just happened to me. Bah, the tea must have been too strong. I simply won't submit to this nonsense, but something strange did indeed happen. Unless my own eyes have betrayed me, I swear I just followed a woman resembling Lady Raftery; she entered a room and closed the door. I called to her just as she shut it. I checked to make sure it wasn't the loo, and I opened the door. I dodged a broom that nearly struck my nose. No Lady Raftery in sight. The room I watched her walk into was a shallow broom closet. Nothing more.

Two

.

Mac O'Malley sat in the Atrium Café of the Tiny Wanderer. He bit his bottom lip and flipped the pages of the leatherbound journal he'd been reading for the last few minutes.

"Edith! Is this all there is? I need to read more of this!"

"Mac. Stop yelling. That is all there is. Pretty neat though, huh?"

"This is so cruel. I need to know what happened to Lady Raftery and even this British detective. Wadsworth was his name?" Mac flipped to the signatory page of the journal and read the ownership line.

"I thought you would get a kick out of that and could use a break from your editor's notes." Edith sipped a cup of tea at the counter just up the steps from Mac's table near the Atrium's centralized fountain.

"Edith. You think this place is really haunted?" Mac scratched the stubble on his chin, then rubbed his bad leg. He was indeed stressed from combing through the laborious notes his editor gave him on the first draft of his heroic memoir detailing his exploits saving lives at a bombing during the Chicago Marathon. His leg ached more than usual today. He didn't want to rely too heavily on his pills either. He dreaded the use of the pills more than the chronic pain and discomfort. Still, his doctor prescribed him the meds in case he needed it. He thought about taking another one before having to dive into another chapter revision. The haunting of the Wanderer helped distract him from his actual work.

"Well, I must say, I have heard some strange stories from the staff over the years. I have never experienced anything myself. It's probably a bunch of hocus pocus. But that journal has been lying around in the back by shipping for years and I combed through it; thought it might interest you." Edith stopped and welcomed a trio of senior women who walked into the café for lunch.

"Bah." Mac thumbed through the journal. Wadsworth felt compelled to write down his journey to America and detail the strange occurrence he had, but then he just stopped the journal and left it here. What happened to him? Why did he leave the journal there and only mustered up one detailed entry? Mac examined the front page of the leatherbound antique. The journal was manufactured in 1919 by Sears and Roebuck in Chicago.

He must have bought the journal upon his arrival to Chicago or even his arrival at the Tiny Wanderer in Geneva. Still, why feel compelled to write this down here at the Wanderer and then leave it?

Edith sat the three women at their table in the corner, nearest the purse department, then walked back towards Mac.

"Edith, can you bring me back by shipping sometime? You said you found this back there. I just want to see exactly where you found it."

"Mac it's nothing special. It is just an old house that was added to the Wanderer in the 50s," Edith said.

"Wait. There was another house added on to the back of the Wanderer? Like an *entire* house?"

"Yes, they just took it out of the ground with hydraulic lifts and moved it here. Pretty ingenious way to preserve the look of the Wanderer rather than adding, like, a big boring warehouse out back."

"Brilliant indeed. I guess I never realized it, but it does look like a house back there. Still, when can we go?"

"Let me get Miguel over here to take these nice ladies' orders and then we can head back there."

"Head back where? We have our bridal registry to build, Mr. O' Malley!" Millie walked into the Atrium Café with a smile and a flourish of her curly silver hair. The magical banker and fiancé of Mac lit up and calmed every room she entered. Her easygoing aura and wry sense of humor proved most satisfying to those who knew her. Mac, obviously, fell for her.

"Oh right, Mills! Hello! Yes, we must do that. Let me just pack up my stuff and we can get started." Mac closed his laptop, gathered the papers of his manuscript, and, of course, made sure to secure Wadsworth's journal in his backpack.

A crack of thunder rattled the patrons of the Atrium Café, followed by a flicker of lights throughout the Wanderer. Suddenly, hard rain pelted the skylight above the fountain in the café.

"Wow, that storm came on fast. Didn't even get an alert about a storm on my phone. Oh, wait what am I talking about; I never get good reception in here." Mac grabbed his backpack.

Another crack of thunder rolled and racked their ears.

"I didn't get any storm warnings or anything either, Mac." Millie examined her phone as well. "Whatever, let's get started. We are meeting Mom and Dad for dinner later."

"Right and you only have about 45 minutes until we close. Get going you two. You're great and all, but I'm not staying late for you." Edith pointed.

"Ha! We shall be quick, Edith. I promise. Can I leave this here behind the counter until we're done?" Mac held up his backpack with one hand and leaned on his cane with the other.

"Of course, you can. You pain in the butt!" Edith shook her head.

"Thanks so much Edith. Shipping house. Soon." Mac dropped his backpack and walked out with Millie.

Three

"Blanche, enough is enough. We don't want to spend the entire trip masquerading as tramps or, frankly, like you." Dotty held her forehead in exasperation. Her curly white hair barely moving if at all with the shake of her head.

"Well, if that's how you feel, Dotty, then bless your heart. Rosalie, I think this would look very flattering on you. Let's at least try it on." Blanche urged her other friend.

"Oh, I don't know, though, I am confident my bosom would look great in that swimsuit. I just don't know how comfortable I would feel is all Blanche. I have to agree with Dotty."

"Rose! It's the 2020s and you still use the word bosom?" Dotty started to smirk, thought about a laugh, but then kept her brow furrowed.

Dotty, Blanche, and Rosalie sat at the corner table of the Atrium Café preparing and planning for their trip to Florida. Blanche held out a clipping from a swimsuit catalog she continued to get via the mail for the last 35 years. Blanche felt age was just a number. Dotty not so much; she was more of a pragmatist. Rosalie was more aloof yet would still find her way to have more of a grounded sense of being much like Dotty. Though, the youthful and adventurous spirit of Blanche did excite her and complimented her well.

"Well, I'll be having way more fun than the two of you anyway, per usual. What time is our flight?" Blanche put away the catalog clipping and sipped the iced tea Miguel had just brought her.

"Our flight leaves at 10 am sharp tomorrow. Let's not be late. The car is supposed to pick us all up at 7 am." Dotty checked the schedule on her cellphone.

"I'm all packed up. I just want to pick up a few more things like a purse from here at the Wanderer. They have such a great collection here." Rosalie perused the menu.

"I could use a sweater. I don't know how warm it will be at night. I will check the weather." Dotty said.

"Oh my, Dotty, you might as well just join the convent. We are still beautiful and able women, we shouldn't just cover ourselves up and wait for the grave." Blanche said.

Dotty rolled her eyes.

Blanche's eyes rolled too, but not in a communicative way. They rolled to the back of her head. She fell off her chair.

Rosalie dropped her menu and screamed.

A loud boom of thunder sounded from above. The hard rain pelted the skylight like before.

"Rose! Stop screaming. We need help in here! Call an ambulance." Dotty stood from her chair and picked Blanche's top half from the café ground.

Rosalie fished her phone from her purse and attempted an emergency call.

"Dotty, my phone doesn't have a good signal."

"Check mine Rose." Dotty nodded toward her phone still on the table in front of her seat.

"Bad signal too, Dot."

"I tried the landline, but that is out too." Miguel the server said, holding the receiver in his hand from the counter.

"Someone in here must have a phone that works. My friend has passed out."

"She still breathing?" Mac O' Malley walked into the room leaning heavily on his cane. Millie was a few paces behind him.

Dotty examined Blanche closely. "I think so."

Mac walked over to Blanche and Dotty.

Millie said, "I just tried my cellphone too. Nothing. An alert did come through, though. A flash flood warning for the area and to stay indoors and get to high ground if need be. It's the storm of the century out there."

"Wonderful, which will make getting an ambulance that much harder." Mac looked at Blanche's mouth. Her mouth seemed filled with drool.

"What is your name, ma'am?"

"Dotty."

"Dotty, can you help me tip her head toward her chest. We have to get this drool out or she may choke on it."

"Yes, whatever we need to do."

Mac supported Blanche's back as Dotty tilted her head forward. Copious amounts of drool and foam bubbled from her mouth.

Mac looked to the table. Three drinks. All iced tea. Only one had the straw inserted.

"Whatever you two do. Do not take a drink of that tea."

"Well, why?" Rosalie asked her hand on her chest in shock from the severity of the situation.

"I think your friend may have been poisoned." Mac monitored Blanche's mouth which seemed to be clear of drool and foam for the time being.

The skylight cracked above from the hard, pelting, relentless, rain. Drips of water began to fall onto the fountain in the middle of the Atrium Café.

Four

"Mac, I personally brewed the tea this morning and would have absolutely no reason to poison it!" Edith walked into the café.

"Who was the last person to handle the carafe of tea?" Mac asked.

"Me." Miguel shook his head and wrung his hands in his apron. "I swear I didn't poison the tea!"

"Edith, round up anyone left in the Wanderer. Search all thirty-six rooms. Millie, can you go with her? I'll stay here." Mac stood up from Blanche's incapacitated body.

"It's close to closing time so there shouldn't be too many people in here, except staff and maybe a few customers." Edith's voice trailed off as she left the room. Millie followed.

"You two know of anyone who might be upset with the three of you? What are your names?" Mac asked.

The tall, sixty-something-year-old said, "I'm Dotty. This is Rosalie. And Blanche is knocked out."

"I don't believe anyone would want to do us harm. Who might you be?" Rosalie asked still holding a hand to her chest. She wore her blonde hair big and curly.

"Right, I'm sorry. I am Officer Mac O'Malley; you might know me from the Chicago Marathon incident."

Dotty and Rosalie just stared at each other. Silence.

"Well, anyway, I'm a retired police officer and am here to help. We just need to make sure her head is propped up in case she starts to foam again."

"I can grab some towels to prop her head up," Miguel said.

"Good idea. She should stay here with us. We can protect her in here until we figure out what is going on. Sheesh, this storm is incredible." Mac felt a raindrop on his neck and looked up toward the freshly cracked skylight.

"Well, Officer, we don't have a clue as to who would want to poison us three. Why? We wouldn't hurt a fly?" Rosalie shook her head.

"I hate flies, Rose, and we aren't that sweet. We are three old ladies who live together on Second Street with my mother. We have some mildly to very annoying neighbors, but then again, who doesn't? I would certainly like to poison them sometimes." Dotty used her hands when she talked as if conducting the local orchestra.

Mac couldn't help but be charmed by these ladies and certainly, wanted to protect and help them further.

"This is rather odd. What about your pasts? Anyone have any dealings with bad guys? Get caught up with the wrong people?" Mac paced the floor and firmly planted his cane as the raindrops started to splash the café floor.

"There was one time in Kansas that some greasers pelted my late husband's car with some rocks," Rosalie answered.

"Rose! How is that pertinent to right now?" Dotty smacked herself in the forehead.

"Haha well, we'll figure out what is going on soon enough. It's sort of what me and my fiancé do."

Millie, as if on cue, walked in with Edith followed by six customers. Six possible suspects.

Five

"No one is to leave this room until I have spoken to all of you. I have reason to believe that the unconscious woman on the floor was poisoned by someone in this building. Until I have vetted and questioned each one of you, no one is to leave this room—"

The sky belched more thunder.

"—not one of you, until we can figure out what happened here. Besides, the biggest midwestern storm since the dust bowl is ravaging the area right now." Mac used his cane to point at the new crew of people entering the Atrium café.

"Sir, I can be of assistance in any way I can." A man with unnaturally blond hair spoke up. He had a long face with coke bottle glasses and dark eyebrows. He was tall, lanky, and rather irritating due to the overwhelming neck beard that spread about his collar line.

"That is awfully kind of you, but I believe I can handle this. I was a cop for many years. Mac looked toward the lanky, awkward man. "What's your name?"

"Fred Forrest. How do you do Mister..." Fred held out his hand for Mac to shake.

"Mac O'Malley. Let's start with Mr. Forrest. Do you know anyone in this room, Mr. Forrest? Dotty, Rose? Do you recognize this man?"

"Never saw him in my life," Dotty said quickly.

Rosalie just shook her head and wiped a tear from her eye as she ran her fingers through Blanche's hair. She didn't even look at Fred.

"I am just passing through on a cross-country trip. Checking out small towns on my way. Geneva is quite the hotspot for small town tourist destinations. It's ranked number 2 in the nation. I just want to help, really. I find it sad that today, even small towns, lack trust in their fellow man. I will be helpful anyway and in any way I can. As you said, there is a bad storm outside. Before I was ushered into here, I looked outside. The streets are flooded, and the rain shows no signs of stopping," Mr. Forrest said.

"Makes driving across country difficult. Okay, okay. Makes sense." Mac didn't like Mr. Forrest. Too quick to make a social commentary about small town trust. A loquacious response for the would-be good Samaritan.

CRACK!

Before Mac could meet the five other strangers, the lights in the Tiny Wanderer flickered then failed. The storm combined with dusk rushed the daytime into slumber. They could barely see a thing. A shrill scream pierced Mac's ear.

"Everyone, relax! I know where the candles are." Edith cried out.

"We probably all have flashlights on our phones, too," Millie suggested.

"Yes, good idea." Mac turned on the flashlight on the phone and began to count people. "Everyone okay? No one left the room, correct? Except for Edith to get some candles. Right?"

"Please, everyone. Take a seat. There are enough chairs in the café to accommodate us all." Millie urged people to sit, guiding them with her cellphone flashlight as well.

Mr. Forrest and the five other customers took seats around the fountain filling with rainwater from the crack in the skylight. Miguel stood by the counter at the entrance to the café and the three women stayed in their area with Blanche still on the floor, breathing slowly.

"Okay, phew, we are all accounted for. Edith brought in six more people. So yes, we are all here."

"Mac and Miguel, help me set up these candles on the tables. Landline phones are out, and cell coverage is non-existent. We will just have to set up shop until the storm passes." Edith held six candlesticks and a bag of long wax candles.

"Will do." Mac walked over and helped Edith prep the candles. The interrogations would soon begin by candlelight in the small cafe. Amongst a murderer.

Six

The candles were set in the middle of the wrought iron tables in the small atrium café. Each of the six customers sat at their own table, their faces dimly lit and menacing. Given the circumstances, Mac thought the reaction was reasonable.

"This is absolutely ridiculous. I can drive home with my truck damnit!" A deep voice rumbled.

Mac turned in the direction of the outburst. "And who might you be?"

"Sergeant Yellow. Served in Afghanistan and don't need you to tell me what I can and can't do." Yellow's face bore deep wrinkles around his eyes and mouth. His skin was taut, nonetheless. Discontent spewed from his pores.

"You don't happen to recognize these ladies and the woman on the floor, do you Sergeant? Thank you for your service, I might add." Mac felt this man's energy from across the room.

Sergeant Yellow shook his head. "I was here shopping for a last-minute gift for my wife's birthday. I have no idea who anyone is. Christ."

"You have no connection to anyone?"

"Jacky, is that you?" Rosalie took a few steps toward Jack Yellow.

"Who are you? I've never seen this woman." Jack looked toward Mac.

"I was friends with your sister, Henrietta, growing up! I am Rosalie Roberts!" Rosalie smiled.

"Oh, shit. Yes, wow, well hello there, Rosalie. I do remember you."

That was where the conversation stopped. Yellow turned away from Rosalie.

Didn't want any part of her, even though they were acquaintances. Mac noted the connection. This was a start.

He scanned the room for more reactions to Rose, Dotty, and Blanche.

"When will this storm end so we can get the hell outta here? Did you ever think that she could just be old and had a stroke?" A crabby, raspy voice rang out from the table next to Yellow.

"Mary! Now you know Blanche was in great shape and just went to the doctor last week." Dotty pointed at the source of the cranky voice. *Mary.*

"I hope she won't die. She owes me after the card game we played last week!" Mary yelled back at Dotty.

"Ladies, please." Millie put her hands up. "No need to yell."

"Mary Rouge probably poisoned her, Officer O'Malley. The nosy, annoying neighbor and overall horrendous human being you see here in front of you." Dotty stood with her hands on her hips.

"Oh please! We all know you weren't Blanche's biggest fan, Dotty!" Mary Rouge fought back. Her perfectly coiffed and curled red hair looked rather devilish in the candlelight.

"Enough is enough. Please ladies, we won't get out of here quicker with endless bickering." Mac scratched the stubble on his chin. A distant connection between Sergeant Yellow and Rosalie and now the fiery Mary Rouge, Blanche's neighbor— it warranted further investigation. Mr. Forrest, the awkward one. Sergeant Yellow, the gruff and mysterious veteran. And Mary Rouge, the neighbor with the strained relationship to the victim.

Three more customers to question.

Seven

Mac remembered a case like this, except it was in a small convenience store. Same deal. Power out. No cameras. A dead body, though, not an incapacitated, live person. It ended easily, as the killer tried to flee the store. Open and shut. No raging storms outside. Just plain and simple.

Time to interrogate the squirrelly guy behind Mr. Yellow.

"Mac, can I talk to you please? Outside of this room?" Millie summoned Mac with her finger.

Mac didn't like being summoned with a finger by anyone. It was annoying and there was work to be done. He followed his fiancé into the darkened stationary department anyway.

"Mac, I love you."

"I love you, too. Is that what you wanted to tell me?"

"You are doing it again. You are jumping to conclusions to have another case to solve. That woman could have passed out for any number of different reasons."

"She was foaming at the mouth, too. The other two didn't drink the tea yet. She was the only one who did. It looks consistent with poisoning to me, Mills. I was a cop and I've seen a lot of shit. Plus, we're just now uncovering connections to her in this store!"

"Mac, Geneva is a small town. People know each other, especially the typical demographic who frequent the Tiny Wanderer: older people. Not sure the card game motive is a strong one."

"That Mary Rouge does seem fierce, though. I understand. I get it. You're right. It would be great if we could get paramedics here, but nothing's working. I even tried the emergency function on my phone. The streets must be flooding. I have *never* heard such hard rain on a roof before. I hope it holds—this is an old building. Scratch that, one time I did drive through a terrible storm with tornadoes on the way to see an ex-girlfriend at U of I. I pulled over at a Waltonmart and you could hear the rain drenching the giant big box store roof, too. I envisioned a huge twister tearing the roof off. It was scary. Legit scary," Mac recounted.

"Mac, I don't really care about ex-girlfriend stories. Still, we should just ride the storm out and stop thinking a murderer is amongst us. That getting through to you?" Millie looked at Mac.

She wasn't getting through. He had a certain look when nothing at all will stop his one-track mind. That look happened in situations like this. A wide-eyed look of hype. Millie was the opposite. She appeared cool and always collected—except around spiders.

"Millie, I just have three more people to talk to and by then, you're right: the storm will have passed, and we can get paramedics in here and figure out what really happened to Blanche. Besides, being over here in the dark is seriously creeping me out. Raftery's ghost is probably around us." Mac turned back in the direction of the café.

"Raftery's what?"

"Raftery's ghost! A young British aristocrat who disappeared in the Wanderer and now haunts the halls and rooms with reckless abandon!"

"Reckless abandon?"

"Sorry, that was a bit too much. Let's get back in there before the ghost gets us for real."

Millie rolled her eyes.

Eight

The chill that ran down Mac's spine did little to comfort him as he found himself back in the Atrium café. Millie may be right. These people could all be innocent shoppers looking for wares for loved ones and a nice gift for themselves or, in the case of the three best friends, a bite to eat. Just a wonderful time together, enjoying company and relaxing until an unfortunate twist of fate and some bad health hit one of them. It all went to hell in a handbasket. Who really would want to harm an older woman? For what reason?

Mac had three more people to interview.

"Professor Marlowe. That's what most people know me as. I teach at North Central College not too far from here." The nervous bald man, looking to be in his late fifties, shifted in the café chair. To Mac, his display of discomfort could mean a few different things. He had to poop. He loathed being in the dark Wanderer on a stormy night. Or, he had something to hide.

"Professor, do you know anyone in this room?" Mac sat across from him. The candle between them flickered.

"No. Well..." Marlowe closed his eyes as if trying to hide.

"Well, what? What brings you to the Wanderer this evening?" Mac pressed.

"My wife is here. She's on the other side of the fountain sitting in a chair. I am not sure she knows I am here. I was here shopping for a surprise gift for her and I didn't want her to know I was here."

Marlowe spoke in a hushed tone. "It will be our 30th wedding anniversary this weekend."

Mac noted the academic's strange behavior. "Ah, okay and rather than say hello to her or comfort her, you're sitting here cowering? Seems a bit suspicious to me there, Professor. Surely your wife would rather you be with her and not hide from her. You know anyone else here, sir?"

"I don't. I do not. Just my wife. Please—*please*, maybe the storm will pass soon and I can leave without her knowing. I already got her gift. " Marlowe brought a bag to the top of the table. "I don't want her to know. I just want it to be a surprise."

"When Edith brought you all in here, how did your wife miss you?" Mac asked.

"I put my hood up and stayed behind her. I couldn't believe she was here."

"This is rather silly."

"Is the woman on the floor okay? Is she alive?"

"She's alive. No worries. Just stay put until this storm rolls through. From the sound of it, looks like we will be waiting a while." Mac secured his cane and walked over to the supposed Mrs. Marlowe on the other side of the café.

Thunder rolled once more. A flash of light lit up the cracked skylight, followed by another roar of thunder. The drips into the fountain increased in frequency and size: what had started as a slow misty, drizzle was now heavy rain.

"Hello there. I am Mac O'Malley and I'm a police officer. I just want to ask you a couple quick questions. What is your name?"

"Kim Marlowe." The frizzy blonde hair and large glasses didn't hide Kim's teary eyes.

"You have nothing to worry about. Once the storm passes, we will all be able to get out of here."

"I know he's here. He doesn't think I know he's here. He's here and I want to kill him."

Nine

Mac cocked his head. The proverbial frog jumped down in his throat. But before he could properly react—

CRACK! BOOM!

The skylight above finally gave way. Shards of glass and metal framing fell onto the fountain, followed by a deluge. The rainwater overwhelmed the fountain and rapidly spread across the floor. The rain and wind wiped out all of the candles in the room.

Darkness.

The hole in the roof widened.

A loud scream resounded off the wrought iron railings, tables, chairs.

The sound of splashing footsteps and chairs screeching on the floor rang out as the café gathering scattered throughout the Tiny Wanderer. Were they looking for safety? Or a safe house from his pursuit?

Mac's once controlled situation now turned to chaos. Blanche was probably still on the floor.

"Dotty, you still there?! Who's still in here with me? Millie?" Mac fumbled for the cell phone in his pocket.

"Mac, I'm with Rosalie in the bag department!"

"Roger that!" Mac yanked his phone from his pocket and illuminated the room with his flashlight. He was the only one left in the room. Rain pelted the area as the roof deteriorated above him. A shingle hit his shoulder. He made sure to use his cane carefully as the rain splashed the floor and began to fill up the café like a tub. He shined the light on Blanche.

"Miguel! Miguel! Can you help me get Blanche off the floor in here? Don't worry Blanche, we got you." Mac knelt, feeling something under his knee, and examined Blanche. He checked for a pulse. He shook his head and pressed harder on her wrist.

"Oh, no, Blanche. Come on now!" Mac dropped her wrist and used the flashlight to see what was under his knee. He noticed a red tinge in the water.

Blood.

Mac used his cane to get up and looked down. A knife. He'd knelt on a knife.

"Oh no."

"Mac, I'm here. Sorry, everything went crazy when the roof caved in. She still breathing?" Miguel came back in with an actual flashlight. The rainfall lit up around him.

"I am afraid not Miguel. She's been murdered."

"Murdered... here?"

"Someone poisoned her earlier and when that didn't work, they used the roof collapse as cover to finish the job."

"Phones are still out. I could go out in the storm and try to reach them?"

"Miguel, the storm will have to stop at some point. The streets are flooded. It's too dangerous and we don't need another death tonight. No, we need to make sure no one leaves. Where can we all gather? We gotta keep this situation contained."

"We can gather in the Gift Galleries and use the fireplace to get warm and dry."

"Good. Good. Let's do a quick sweep and get everyone back in here. There were eleven of us in the café. There will be ten of us in the Gift Galleries. Let's do this Miguel."

Ten

Kim Marlowe. The last person Mac interrogated. She outright admitted murderous intent. Mac had to find her fast.

And now.

"Kim! Kim!" Mac left the flooded Atrium Café and headed into the Accessories department, his flashlight thrust out in front of him. The likelihood she would respond to his calls was improbable. Only if she wanted to be clever and hide her guilt...or not.

"Yes, yes, I am in here next to some kitchen towels!" Kim yelled from one of the thirty-six rooms of the Tiny Wanderer.

"Stay right there! On my way!" Mac made his way through the Linens and Lighting section and to Housewares. He knew the Wanderer well.

He found the blonde hair and glasses of one Mrs. Marlowe.

"We need to finish our conversation, Kim. Why do you want to kill your husband?" Mac attempted to dry his face with his wet leather jacket sleeve. It didn't really work as well as he'd hoped.

"I swear, I did not poison that woman. I would rather poison my husband. After 28 years of marriage, he's cheating on me. That is why, but I haven't done it. Today he said he was working. Grading mid-terms. I followed him here and he was with *her*. Doting on her and willing to get her gifts. Makes me sick." Kim took off her glasses and rubbed the bridge of her nose.

"Is she here now? Who is she?"

"Yes, she was here with him before splitting off with the woman who got poisoned and her friend."

"Officer O'Malley! Officer O'Malley! Come quick!" The deep voice of Mr. Forrest resounded from the room Mac had just passed through.

"On the way. Kim, you'd better just come with me." Mac pointed with his cane toward the lighting gallery. No light but a room filled with lamps and linens. When illuminated, the ceiling bore intricately painted floral and pastel designs filled with pinks and greens. But it was a pleasant, calming room no more.

"Robin and I found her on the floor. We think she may be dead." Mr. Forrest walked Mac and Kim to a counter on the opposite side of the walking lane through the Wanderer's rooms. Forrest breathed heavily and was clearly upset.

There she lay.

Dotty.

Dotty in the Lighting gallery with a candle-stick next to her.

Mac maneuvered his phone light around her body. Severe trauma to the head in the form of deep contusions and bumps. "No one touch anything!"

A woman stood behind the counter, peering down over the body. "I'm Robin Billingsley. I just started working here in the toy department. I left my purse behind this counter and when I came to pick it up, I found her here."

"Mr. Forrest said you both found her. Is he lying?" Mac pressed, shining his light right in her face.

"No, sorry, he was with me. We were sitting by each other in the café and left at the same time in all the panic."

"Fair enough. Come out from there and be careful not to touch anything. Someone bludgeoned Dotty on the head—this is a crime scene."

Miguel's voice burst from another room in the darkness. "Please, if everyone could follow me and Edith into the Gift Galleries section. There is a fireplace there. We can all keep warm and have light until the storm passes!"

Mac said, "Go ahead and follow his voice and meet me by the fireplace."

Robin Billingsley didn't react with the typical emotion upon seeing a dead body. Mac had no idea what Robin may or may not have seen in her life, but still. A rather odd non-reaction. Noted.

Kim Marlowe said she was by a bunch of towels in the Housewares section of the store. She would have had to pass through Linens and Lighting to get to Housewares. Would she have had time to track Dotty down in the dark and beat her head in with a candlestick—then flee to Housewares?

And further: why be so forthcoming with her feelings if she wanted to conceal her guilt as one would naturally do? Maybe she didn't care. Maybe she was so angry with her husband and his mistress that she just didn't care anymore. The answers lay in the Gift Galleries section where hopefully Miguel had stoked a strong fire. The cold, damp room with a cold, dead body did little to comfort Mac.

The sound of a steady stomp emanated from the ceiling above.

The bending of floorboards and the usual creaks and squeaks befitting an old house like the Wanderer lasted more than Mac would have liked. Something was up there.

Edith and Miguel did a sweep of the whole store earlier. Did they miss someone? Was there even a floor above the Linens and Lighting section?

"Lady Raftery?" Mac muttered to himself as he sprayed the ceiling with light from his phone.

The stomping ceased.

"Oh hell no." Mac moved as fast as his cane would support him. He weaved through the Bath and Body department and on to the Gift Galleries. Shadows from the fireplace's flames danced on the walls. Unlike everywhere else he'd been, the Gift Galleries was filled with warm bodies. Alive and mildly well, given the circumstances.

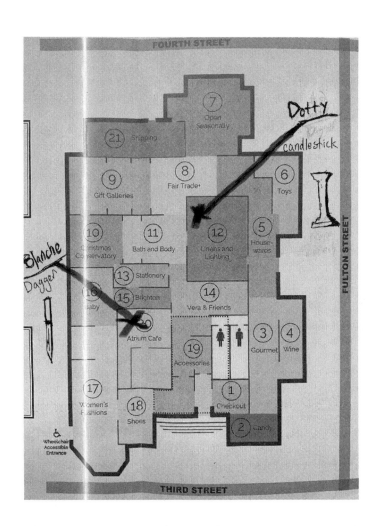

Eleven

The Gift Galleries was right next to the Christmas Conservatory and held an overflow of clearance items from the Christmas section. The fireplace and mantle were painted white; the walls a dark blue. The room held lots of different merchandise and a variety of goods. Many necklaces placed on white cloth heads with blank faces. Other rings and bracelets were displayed along the walls. It was a mash-up of gifts and people waiting a storm out and under investigation. Millie heard the gangly Mr. Forrest loudly blab, "My god, another body. The other woman now—they're just piling up around here."

Millie glared at him, "That's rather insensitive, don't you think?"

The good witch consoled Rosalie as best she could. Dotty and Blanche. Two of Rosalie's best friends had been murdered in a very short span of time. All Millie could do was hold her as she wept. She couldn't help but feel awful for Rosalie.

"I can't imagine how you feel, Rosalie. I am so sorry. We'll figure out who did this." Millie looked up and scanned the room. Someone in this room killed them. That sent a chill down Millie's spine and rage filled her as well. "You're safe with me."

Where the hell was Mac?

Rosalie buried her face in Millie's shoulder and gripped her tightly in shock, fear, and grief all rolled into one, Millie surmised. Her empathic instincts worked at full tilt this stormy evening.

Seriously, where the hell is he? A tinge of anxiety roiled her stomach.

Millie looked in the direction of the Christmas Conservatory. A display of wreaths and small trees blocked her sightline. The firelight only reached so far. She thought she heard something in that direction.

A phone's flashlight bobbed.

There he was. He moved fast.

"Are we all here? Edith! Miguel! Everyone accounted for?" Mac entered the room with a roaring voice. Typical.

"Yes, the Marlowes are here. Rosalie. Millie. Mr. Forrest. Robin. Miguel. Mary Rouge. Sergeant Yellow and you and me. Yes, we are all here." Edith pointed at each person as she took roll.

Mac stared at each suspect in turn. "Under no circumstances, does anyone leave this room. If you must pee, do so in the corner. We need to wait this storm out. Together. That is key."

"I was worried about you and then you come in here so loud, barking orders and I want you to leave again. Take it easy Mac," Millie said.

"I don't take orders from a cripple cop." Sergeant Yellow grumbled.

"Where were you after everyone scattered from the Atrium, Yellow?" Mac pointed his cane at him.

"I came in here, actually. I was the first one in here. Don't accuse me of your bullshit." Sergeant Yellow huffed and puffed and flicked Mac's cane away.

"Hey! We need to calm down and just wait this out." Millie interjected. Rosalie still clung to her.

"I don't want to be in here with a killer!" Mary Rouge looked ready to hyperventilate. Her eyes were wide. Face pale. Breathing shallow.

"Yes, we should take our chances in the storm versus being stuck in here with a murderer!" Sergeant Yellow seconded Mary's sentiments.

"We can't let you leave." Miguel stepped up and flanked Edith and Mac.

"Leaving would be an admission of guilt. All of you are obviously flight risks. Unless someone wants to confess right now and make things easy. Because right now, I have a stabbed woman in the café and another woman with her head bashed in Linens and Lighting. Whether you like it or not, you are all murder suspects. I will bring the full might of the local and state police down on you and your families if you attempt an escape." Mac didn't move from his spot and leaned on his cane with a commanding stature. He braced both hands against the curved top and planted his feet as firm as his resolve.

Millie nodded her head.

"How do we know you didn't kill them O'Malley?" Professor Marlowe stood alone on the opposite side of the room from Millie.

"I was in the room with—" Mac looked visibly upset. Ready to fight.

"You're right. We are all suspects." Millie interjected. She gave Mac a look of both comfort and shrewdness. Millie knew Mac let Marlowe make him angry. She had to defuse it before Mac lost control of the room.

"Mac took a deep breath. "Fair enough. We are all suspects."

Twelve

"Millie, could you come with me?" Mac looked at his fiancé.

"Yes. Be right there. Rose, I will be back in a few." Millie smiled at her; it took a few moments, but Rosalie finally let her go and instead leaned on the fireplace mantle.

Mac led her into the Christmas Conservatory, the room next to the Gift Galleries. He sprayed his flashlight around the room. It felt eerie with darkened Christmas trees and ornaments that just collected dust after not selling at Christmastime. He looked at an owl ornament with a Santa hat on. Its yellow eyes burrowed into his soul. Why did it freak him out so much? He remembered his grandfather telling him spooky stories about an evil owl that hooted at night in the tree next to his bedroom window. That was why. After all these years. Still frightening.

Mac checked the rest of the room. Clear—though, with all the Christmassy goods packed into the room, it was impossible to be 100% sure.

"Millie, we have to regroup here. This is getting out of hand. In the span of a few minutes, two people were brutally killed by someone—or something—in the Wanderer." Mac held the flashlight at Millie.

"Mac, for the love of God, put the flashlight down." Millie shielded her face with her arms.

"Oh sorry, sorry." Mac put the torch down, but it still gave off enough light for them to see each other. A flash of lightning then illuminated the room once more.

Thunder.

"Gosh, could this night be any more of a horror movie?! Sheesh!" Mac shook his head.

"Mac, let's just work through this. You are right: we need to collect ourselves and figure out what to do."

"Do storms really last this long?" Mac asked.

"Mac."

"Okay, right, right. Whoever or whatever it was that killed Dotty and Blanche did it quickly and with weapons they could find in the area."

Millie said, "You need to catch me up here, buddy. I was with Rosalie when we scattered from the Atrium café. She had to find the bathroom, so I brought her there and when she was done, we listened to Miguel and came to the Gift Galleries."

"When everyone scattered in hysterics from the ceiling cave-in, I stood pat to see to Blanche when

I found a knife next to her and bloodied water. Think *Jaws*, but on the floor in the café. Someone in the commotion and darkness was cold enough, swift enough, to finish her off."

"The poison didn't work so the murderer had to be sure she was dead. Wow. Shrewd yet skillful." Millie shrugged.

"Then said murderer followed Dotty into the Linens and Lighting room—or lured her behind the counter—and killed her with the candlestick. Both weapons were left next to the victims."

"Gloves. Gloves would need to be worn, right? You can't just leave fingerprints on murder weapons next to the victims. We should search for gloves. Maybe search everyone for gloves in the Gift Galleries. Do you have any ideas on who it might be? Why are the group of friends being targeted?" Millie began to pace.

"Don't walk around too much. It's still super dark in here. I was trying to string together connections to Blanche, and we do have a disgruntled neighbor in Mary Rouge. A scorned wife, Kim Marlowe, suspected that one of the three friends—Rosalie, Dotty, not Blanche—was the mistress of one dorky Professor Marlowe. As Kim was about to tell me which one it was, Rosalie or Dotty, we were interrupted by Mr. Forrest yelling about dead Dotty's body. Sorry, that was in bad taste."

"It was. Go on. Do you think Kim Marlowe did it?"

"I suppose there is a very slight chance that she could have pulled it off, but I don't think so. After the café ceiling collapsed, I found her far away in the Housewares section of the store. The timing doesn't add up. Besides, why would she kill two of them when only one of them was having an affair with her hubs? She denied killing anyone, but made it clear she wanted to kill her husband for cheating on her."

"Fair enough. She could still be a suspect. But you're assuming the murders are related. They could be separate motives from two different people." Millie paced and ignored Mac's previous directive.

"This is very true. I also didn't like Robin's reaction to Dotty's dead body. She was cold and not at all rattled. No one in this place, besides Edith and Miguel, are clear in my book. We must tread carefully. We should search for the gloves while we are out here. But we also need to search upstairs. I heard someone walking upstairs. Stomping rather. I mean, it also could very well be... you know..." Mac put his palms up and looked at Millie.

"Mac. There is no ghost in here killing people. What did you call it? Simon's ghost?"

"Simon's ghost?! Where the heck did you get that? I said Lady Raftery's ghost. Not Simon's ghost." Mac was disgusted. Perhaps overly so.

"Sorry, maybe I said that because I was listening to 'Sweet Caroline' earlier in the car. Either way, it's no ghost. Are we just supposed to use our phone flashlight while we search this place?"

"Yes, and my phone is almost dead. Not exactly the best night for us to make our wedding registry, huh? Why does this always happen to us? Your phone charged?"

"Yes." Millie fished her phone from her pocket and examined the screen. "A little below half though."

"Let's do this. We shouldn't split up. I don't want to lose you in this labyrinth. You would think I would know this place by now since I wrote my entire book here, but I still get confused from time to time." Mac admitted.

"You are dumbish."

"You sounded like your Mom there. Like, almost exactly like Beck."

"Shut up. Now let's go check out upstairs."

"Edith! Miguel! Keep everyone in the room. We're gonna do a quick sweep of the Wanderer!" Mac yelled toward the Gift Galleries.

"We have this under control. Don't let the ghosts spook you!"

"Very funny!"

Thirteen

Mac and Millie made their way through the Conservatory and into Bath and Body. Each step filled Mac's chest with dread. The creaking floor. The pelting rain. The thud of his cane followed by his feet. Millie's footsteps. Two bodies lay dead on the floor of a place he loved; he needed to find the killer and fast. Maybe the killer wasn't in the Gift Galleries. Maybe he or she remained hidden upstairs in some secret office room. Maybe the stomping above him that he had heard earlier denoted panic and guilt for killing two older, presumably innocent, women... or just the haphazard attempt to flee.

They made their way through the narrow Stationery section filled with cards and pens and to the bathroom area and handbag department. They held hands, Mac noted how sweaty Millie's hands were. The couple used their flashlights to create a wide field of vision. Surprisingly, the flashlight power cast a broad field of view—maybe seven to ten feet.

Again, the floorboards seemed to creak louder the more they walked. Further and further away from the gallery; the gallery with a warm fire. Mac didn't realize how wet and cold he was in the dead air of the powerless Wanderer.

"Okay, the stairs are up ahead. Mills, earlier I was reading a journal written by a guy who saw a woman walk into a broom closet in here and just disappear. He couldn't find her. She was just gone. Just gone."

"Mac, I admit, this place is old, and it is ripe for the imagination to think a place as historic as the Wanderer is haunted. But I assure you, it's not. I'm a witch, with magical powers and everything. Ghosts just simply don't exist. Now, I'll head up the stairs first." Millie let go of Mac's hand to grab the stairwell railing.

The stairs were placed at the traditional entrance to the Wanderer. The front Third Street entrance, not the yellow awning-laden side entrance on Fulton that Mac used. Customers opened the door and the stairs greeted them. And like most stairwells built in the late 1800s, the staircase was narrow and curved near the top so one couldn't see the upstairs without climbing the steps.

"Millie, don't get too far ahead of me." Mac watched Millie climb the stairs with ease and rued the day he lost full control of his leg. Forever with a cane.

"I won't. Besides, there probably isn't anything up here anyway. Maybe a raccoon trying to keep dry." Millie charged up the steps and reached the second floor before Mac cleared the second step.

Mac kept on climbing the steps. He'd made it to the middle of the stairs.

His phone lost charge.

Darkness.

"Shit. Millie! Can you come back here? My phone died."

No answer.

"Millie?"

Mac climbed the steps as fast as he could. Maybe his eyes would adjust.

"Millie!" He reached the top floor and reached out for the wall to help guide him through the upstairs. He couldn't see.

"Millie! I can't see a damn thing! Stop foolin' around!"

Nothing. Just the wind howling and more rain. *The incessant rain.*

"Millie, I'll be right back. I'll get a flashlight from Miguel and I will be right back. I can just yell to them."

From below, the sound of a slamming door beat against the wall.

Slam!

Slam!

Boom!

The storm blew the door open. Someone entered or... Lady Raftery's ghost didn't like Mac and Millie in her domain.

Fourteen

------- ------------------------------

"There's no defense for walks, Millie. Remember that." Hank said.

"Dad. I know. You have made that very clear."

A mischievous grin graced Hank's face. "That's okay. Remember to give it a good rotation and just let her rip. We will worry about your form later, kiddo."

Millie always felt very stressed when learning something new. This was the very first time she learned how to pitch a softball and she always felt intense failure if she didn't do some-

thing well right away. This would be no different.

She let another ball release from her hand. It
sailed over her father's head.

"Sorry Dad. I just... can we take a break?"

"Millie, we just started. Give it a few more
tries before you head in. It's beautiful outside.
Besides, I don't really want to have to go home
and be around your mother any more than I have
to." Hank laughed.

"I get it. I totally get it. She made me hit into
the blue tarp all morning." Millie rolled her
eyes and laughed.

Hank threw Millie the ball back. "Okay, give
it a few more tries. Come on."

"Fine."

Millie rotated her entire arm in a windmill,
loosening her shoulder and pitching arm. The
dusk sunlight cast an orange glow on the dirt
field below her feet. The smell of cigarette

smoke from the game right before this mo-

ment still permeated the air around the field.

She looked to Dad behind home plate, his glove

ready to receive yet another errant pitch.

Millie smiled.

Millie awoke in darkness. She could hear tor-

rential rain above her head. She searched for her

phone. The good witch fished through her pockets

and purse as blind as a bat for her phone to illumi-

nate her environment.

No luck.

She felt around the room with her hands out.

The wall was close. Very close. She moved her

hands along the wall—another wall. Then another.

A very small room.

"A closet? I'm in a closet? Mac!" She yelled.

Millie knocked on all the walls until she found

the door. The hollow sound of wood opposed to

plaster helped her. She felt around for the door-

knob.

"There it is." Millie grabbed the doorknob and twisted as hard as she could.

It wouldn't budge. Did someone lock her in? Was it just stuck? There wasn't enough room to use her powerful legs, otherwise, she would have kicked the damn door down by now.

"Hello? Let me out!" Millie tried once more to get through to the outside world, but it was no use. The door wouldn't budge. She must have been in some attic closet, some cubbyhole room, in the labyrinthine Tiny Wanderer.

She listened for someone on the other side of the door. Nothing. She heard nothing. Her seclusion and solitary confinement had been confirmed.

She didn't have her wand either. She would easily bust herself out with a quick spell and flick of her wrist. She thought of the dream of her father and pitching to him after a game. She could really use his help right now. Anyone's help.

But wait—some spells worked without the assistance of a wand. If a witch lost her wand, there was a way to summon the wand. The problem was ensuring that the wand could find her. The magic of Seeking or Seeking Magic as it was mostly named, was finicky and not exact. The wand could essentially stop in front of the Tiny Wanderer—out on the front lawn—thinking it made it to Millie. She needed someone to ensure the wand's delivery. That would require even more magic and could be risky...but given the circumstances, she needed to get out and help Mac.

Frankly, she needed to protect him from himself.

The killer could still be in this building. The killer could have stuffed her in this closet. How the hell did she even get here in the first place?

Fifteen

"Miguel, I need your flashlight. My phone died and Millie is upstairs. I have to get back there." Mac ordered as he entered the warm fireplace-lit Gift Galleries section where the rest of the suspects and Wanderer crew waited the storm out.

"Here you go. We have plenty of candles and other phones if need be. Hopefully the power will be back up soon. Find anything yet?" Miguel handed Mac the flashlight.

"I am afraid not. I should have just grabbed this from you before I left the room earlier. I knew my phone was dying. Gah, no, we're going to continue our search. The front door swung open though. Thought that was strange. I closed it."

"Mac, that is odd," Edith spoke up from next to Rosalie, both huddled together in front of the fire. "I know the storm is bad, but I locked that door myself earlier. Better check it for any signs of forced entry."

"Will do. That is odd." Mac scanned the room and did a quick census.

"Everyone is here." Miguel counted with Mac.

"The storm is strong, but last time I looked there were no tornado warnings. Just flash flood warnings. I will head over there." Mac clicked the button on the flashlight.

Mr. Forrest raised his hand as if in class. "Do you need someone to go with you?"

"No, best to keep everyone here. Right, Mac?" Edith said.

"Yes. I got this."

Mac walked backed through the Fair-Trade Section and back to the front of the building at the Third Street entrance. There were times during his career as a cop that Mac felt a sense of chaos and not control; that maybe he wasn't going to get the bad guy this time. That the criminal was always a step or two ahead. That feeling of doubt pervaded his heart this night. Something didn't feel right about the entire situation. Two dead bodies. Two victims. A room full of suspects. No power. No respite from the rain. *A perfect storm.*

The killer was smart enough not to leave. There were too many witnesses and they'd been together too long: anyone could give a detailed description. It was *possible* that Edith and Miguel missed someone on their initial sweep, but too many connections had been established to think the killer fled.

Who opened the front door though?

Mac made it to the entrance with ease and quickly shined the flashlight on it. Still closed. The interior view of the door looked clean of foul play...but the jamb showed cracks near the handle. Mac unlocked the bolt and opened the door. The front looked much worse. A serpentine crack ran out from the stress of a crowbar, or some other instrument used to force entry.

Someone did enter the Wanderer and that someone was most likely who he'd heard stomping around earlier. Where Millie was currently searching!

"Millie!" Mac turned around and hopped up the curved stairwell.

He reached the landing and looked down a narrow hall with multiple doors. Millie was nowhere to be found.

"Millie!" Mac yelled again.

No answer. Mac counted four doors: two on the left side of the hall, one on the right, and one in the center of the hall where it ended.

A roll of thunder pounded his ears in rhythm with his heart. Something about the hallway didn't seem right. There was floral wallpaper adorning the walls that, with light, probably looked vibrant and colorful. In the glow of the LED flashlight bulb, though, it looked dark and menacing. Like when Snow White got lost in the woods fleeing the Huntsman: creeping, shifting, somehow changing shape just outside his peripheral vision. Mac's overactive imagination did little to comfort him. He needed to find Millie and the Tiny Wanderer's newest patron.

Sixteen

Mac took a deep breath. He gripped his cane with his right hand and the flashlight in his left hand, well aware that someone could jump out at him at any moment. The closest door was to the left of him. He wished he'd had his gun with him. Door breaches were one of the most dangerous exercises one learned in the academy and utilized in real police work. Mac remembered the sweat beading from his forehead and the sting in his eyes as he held a shotgun in position: ready to enter a battery suspect's home. He never felt so scared and hyped in his life. Though, his current situation did match the intensity.

Raftery's Ghost could very well be up here along with the mystery guest. Millie had to be up here—and it shouldn't be difficult to find her. There weren't many places to go or hide.

He opened the first room door. A rather unkempt, small powder room. Some toilet paper was rolled up in a ball on the floor and the faucet loudly leaked with an even, albeit dripping, beat.

Nothing. No one in here.

Mac closed the door and moved on further down the hall. He looked to the singular door on the right and entered.

An office. It had to be Edith's office. It was tidy and practical, with a smattering of papers on a large, glass-topped, oak desk. Her computer was open, but the power light wasn't blinking. It probably lost power like everything else in here. There were no chairs in front of the desk, likely in an effort to discourage visitors who wasted time. A plain, well-worn office chair was behind the desk; a denim jacket draped on the back. What caught Mac's attention most, though, were the pictures on the walls: the Tiny Wanderer throughout the years. He would have loved to stay and examine everything in this room, but he had Millie to look after.

The sound of a hinge creaked Mac turned and walked back into the hallway. He shined the light on the two remaining doors. The one on the left remained closed. The one at the end of the hall had opened just a crack.

The source of the creaking hinge indeed.

Mac gulped air. He fought his heart to slow its thumping beat. He needed to remain calm. Who opened that door?

"Millie. I swear if you are messing with me..."

The door opened even more. Someone could have been on the other side of it, toying with him. Probably his beautiful fiancé.

Mac edged closer to the door. "Millie. Come on. If you're in there just come out. We have to figure out what's going on."

"Mac! Get down here fast!" A loud voice boomed from below. "Hurry!"

"Oh God!" Mac jumped; he dropped the flashlight. It hit the ground with a loud clatter and rolled forward, the beam illuminating the open door at the end of the hallway.

It was open. He couldn't make out what was in the room beyond it but in the threshold—

A creepy woman-like figure stood in the doorway.

Mac shook his head. He couldn't believe his eyes.

"Mac! Come quick! It's Mr. Forrest!" Edith yelled.

"I'm coming. I'm coming." Mac picked up the flashlight and turned away from the door in shock and wonderment. He wanted to get far, far away from the creepy woman—but he was still worried about Millie.

He hesitated and shook his head. He had to find Millie.

"Mac! He's been shot!"

Seventeen

"Millie! Millie! Just stay where you are. I'll be right back!" Mac turned around and headed back down the staircase to Edith.

She was waiting at the base of the stairs. "Hurry, come quick!"

"What happened now?" Mac trailed Edith back through the halls and to the Gift Galleries section of the store.

"He was shot in the shoulder and slumped down immediately. He passed out, but he's still breathing." Edith sounded rattled. She gripped a lit candlestick in her hand.

Thunder roared from outside once more. It felt like it rattled the Wanderer's walls.

"Jeez, when will this storm let up?" Mac limped along with his cane.

Edith said, "Mac, not gonna lie, maybe it would be safer to just brave the storm and get far away from the Wanderer."

"Edith. I understand. We can't, though, we need everyone here. The storm will pass and then we can get Vince and the GPD here. For now, we stick together and stay here."

"Where's Millie?"

"Upstairs somewhere, but not responding when I call to her. Add that to the list of problems we have here." Mac entered the Gift Galleries. Mr. Forrest lay unconscious and face down on the floor in front of the fireplace. Mary Rouge, Yellow, Rosalie, The Marlowes, and Miguel huddled around him.

"Gimme some room here, guys. Thanks." Mac examined the wound in Forrest's right shoulder. He would probably lose the use of his shoulder and the arm, but he would live. That meant whoever wanted him shot had missed the mark.

"Where was he standing when the shot happened, Edith?"

"He was standing with his back toward the Fair-Trade section. He was the only one on that side of the room. He fell forward," Edith explained. "And all of us were here and accounted for."

"Which means there is someone else in the Wanderer with us. That explains the door being opened earlier. Someone else is in here with us." Mac looked around the room for any other shots or even the bullet.

"Spread out everybody. I need to examine the floor and the room." Mac used the flashlight to look at the floor: it was splattered with blood from Forrest's shoulder. On the floor near where Edith said Forrest stood, Mac noticed some white powder—bits of drywall.

He tilted the flashlight up; a bullet hole in the ceiling. Two shots were fired. One in his shoulder and the other in the ceiling. A professional killer knew to double-tap the trigger to put a man down. The second shot missed and hit the ceiling—but how and why? He had assumed it was a professional, but that kind of bumble could have been an amateur who never fired a gun ever before. There was no quick judgement because everyone was in the room when Forrest was shot, according to Edith.

"Edith, you said it came from this way. This is Fair Trade." Mac shined the light down the hall west of the Gift Galleries section. The fire's light didn't reach that far down the hall.

"Miguel, want to take that flashlight you got and join me?" Mac walked further into the darkness of the Fair-Trade section of the Wanderer.

Right in the direction where the shots were fired.

Eighteen

Mac tried to remain calm. Keep a clear head. He worried about Millie still missing in action and now he had to make sense of the shots fired. Did the person who shot Mr. Forrest *mean* to shoot him? Or were the shots intended for someone else, like Rosalie? She was the last friend alive in the group of three friends. Was she the target?

"Miguel, where was Rosalie when Forrest got shot? Do you recall?" Mac asked.

"She was sitting on the floor with her back against the side wall."

"So, she was to the side. Not in the line of fire at all."

"No. She wasn't near him. The shooter would have had to have been a terrible shot if he was aiming for her."

"Someone wanted to kill Mr. Forrest. Why?" Mac hobbled further into Fair Trade with Miguel. Mac couldn't surmise what made Fair Trade different from Gift Galleries. He noticed some local memorabilia. Geneva mugs and coasters, Fox River Valley town gear, and other assorted merchandise. He also noticed something very strange: the further he walked into Fair Trade, the more the strange structure revealed itself.

"Miguel, is this a normal display?" Mac pointed his flashlight.

Miguel directed his beam to the same spot. "This is not normal. We didn't do this."

Mac and Miguel looked at a huge barricade made of tables, shelving units, and chairs.

"This is interesting. Any idea as to why this would happen?"

Miguel's eyes were wide with fear. "No Mac. This is strange."

"We need to move around this and keep looking. Did you hear furniture being moved around in the last hour or so?"

"No. All this furniture is used here in Fair Trade, but it wasn't like this when we did our last sweep."

"This would have made a lot of noise." Mac grimaced. "Are you sure?"

"No. Mac, I have no idea how this happened. We didn't hear this."

"Okay then. Here we go. Let's make our way through this and see why we're being blocked." Mac walked toward a chair stacked at an awkward angle on a blue tablecloth topped card table. He eased the chair to the ground and walked over to Miguel, patting his back. "We need to look for some shell casings and the shooter, Miguel. Come on. We can do this."

"This isn't the first time strange things like this have happened here, Mac." Miguel put his hand to his mouth and rubbed his chin.

"You think Raftery's ghost did this? Anyone could have done this, Miguel. Stacking furniture is not work exclusive to ghosts."

"They're trying to keep us away from this area for a reason. Maybe we should listen."

"Is there another way into this area? Can't we go through Bath and Body, Linens and Lighting, to Housewares and around?"

"*You* can."

"Miguel. Please."

Nineteen

Mac and Miguel moved through the darkened rooms and hallways of the storm-drenched Tiny Wanderer. They made it to Linens and Lighting without issue. Mac shined his flashlight toward Dotty's body behind the cash register counter. She was still there. No one had tampered with her body. It will be key for the investigation when Vince could finally make it here with the GPD to conduct a proper investigation.

Miguel walked a few paces in front of Mac. "We're blocked here too."

"The entrance to Housewares is blocked! What is going on?!" Mac's frustration grew. A stack of boxes, a couple of chairs, and shelving blocked them off from a significant portion of the Tiny Wanderer and the Fulton Street entrance.

"Well, damnit Miguel, we need to get in there!" Mac poked the makeshift barrier with his cane. The barrier didn't budge.

"I tried Mac. There's no way we're moving this stuff. We're cut off from this side. It's like someone nailed it all down to the floor."

"What the hell is going on? And where the heck is Millie?!"

***

Millie needed to do something. She had no concept of time and being stuck in a pitch-black closet for this long did little to comfort her. Her wand was really the only way out of here. It was a risk she needed to take.

"Wand Seeketh." Millie spoke the words aloud. She didn't know if it would work, but she had to try. She needed only to say it once. She struggled to remember where she'd left the wand. Probably her apartment.

Maybe.

***

Hank Paderson stood looking out the front window and to the street. The drainage system of WitchHazel Court could not keep up with the torrential rain. A vast puddle—now practically a lake—nearly covered the entire cul-de-sac. Only the grassy and muddy center of the roundabout showed.

Hank hoped that Becca would stay at work until the storm subsided. He was bummed that dinner with Millie and Mac would probably be canceled.

Hank's phone vibrated in his swishy, athletic pants pocket.

It was Becca.

Hank sighed then answered. "Hello."

"Don't sound so happy to hear from me, Hank." Becca's acerbic tone filled Hank's ear.

"What do you want now, dear?"

"I was wondering if I should get some chicken to bring home and invite them over? What do you think? Have you heard from them? I've tried calling, but there's no answer and no texts back either."

"Sure, if we get a hold of them. They should come over if it's safe to drive." Hank looked at his white pick-up truck, still well above the waterline of Lake Cul-de-sac, when he realized that Becca wasn't even listening.

She kept rambling. "I will order ahead. How do you spell Popeyes?"

"Pop and then eye, Beck. How do you not know that?" Hank shook his head. He heard a crash from behind him in the kitchen.

"Pop and then 'I,' the letter 'I'. Got it." Becca squawked through Hank's receiver. "That isn't it idiot!"

"No Beck! P–O–P–E–Y–E–S. Jeez! Who's the real idiot here?" Hank walked toward the kitchen. He saw Millie's wand hopping around the kitchen like a blind frog. It knocked over Hank's water cup.

"Hank! Stop it. Don't even think for a second that you're smarter than me. I'll get some food. Byeee." Becca hung up.

Hank, a heck of an athlete in his youth, grabbed for the wand that kept bouncing around the granite countertop of the kitchen island. He gripped it and it pulled away like a dog on a leash. Okay, he'd let it lead him then, at least, to an extent.

He kept a strong grip.

It brought him back to the window where he'd previously stood. It tapped on the glass.

Hank felt an incredible sense of both wonder, fear, and a tinge of empowerment. He felt different when grabbing the wand.

Millie's wand kept tapping the glass.

It clearly wanted out.

Twenty

Hank pulled the wand toward the front hall and grabbed his shoes and jacket. He felt more powerful with each second that passed. He knew that willpower was a key component in wielding magic, as he'd observed from his magical family. He, being the only one without natural powers, often was left on the sidelines while Becca and his kids practiced and mastered the magical arts.

Hank would pick up Becca's wand and try to perform magic, but the wand never responded. He just didn't have the power. Now, though, at this moment, Millie's wand responded to him.

"Hang on! Let me get my shoes and jacket on!" Hank yelled at the wand. The wand pointed toward the front door as if it was urging him once more to leave. Hank wondered if Millie might be in trouble.

"Stop," Hank commanded the wand. It stopped moving. Hank sat on the stairs and put his shoes on and then his jacket, all the while never letting go of the wand.

He was ready to go. Holding the wand up to his face, he said with a stern look, "Okay, lead the way."

He opened the door and, together, he and Millie's wand headed out into the night storm. The yellow glow of streetlights showed the sideways rain that pounded the pavement, grass, and streets.

Hank trudged over the grass in a direct line toward his pick-up truck. For some reason, he felt comfortable talking to the wand. "We won't be able to drive through this, even with my pick-up truck!"

The wand smacked him on the side of the head.

"Ow! What the heck?!" Hank rubbed his head with his left hand.

The wand started bobbing in his right hand as if urging Hank to direct its magic.

Hank pointed the wand at his white pick-up truck. Sparks of blue and gold shot from the wand and surrounded the truck.

Hank grinned. Magic had a new name: Hank Paderson.

The white pick-up lifted off the ground and hovered. The water from the wheel-wells drained and dripped.

"Whoa." Hank pulled the wand toward him. The driver's door opened ready for him to fly the truck.

He wiped the rain off his forehead and headed to the truck; it tipped toward him, inviting him in for a ride. Hank grabbed the interior door handle and climbed in. His heart pounded. He wasn't exactly sure how to fly his truck. Yet, the overwhelming sense of fun seemed to overpower his worry.

The wand escaped his grasp.

The windows were fogged up. Hank tried to wipe the windshield with his sleeve.

Wand started drawing on the side passenger window.

Hank read the message aloud. "To Millie."

Wand then tapped the windshield indicating the direction it wanted Hank to go.

"Let's roll. Buckle... whatever."

Hank turned the keys to the ignition, turned on the defroster and the high beams, and then took a hold of the wheel. The truck flew into the rainy night sky.

To Millie.

Twenty-One

Mac and Miguel scoured every nook and cranny for a way to the Fulton Street side of the Wanderer. They were blocked at every entrance, from the Checkout area at the front and back to Fair Trade. It was the same formation of blockade: immovable furniture and knick-knacks stacked to block the way.

Mac turned away from the Checkout room in disgust. He shined his flashlight up the curved stairwell to where he'd seen Millie last. It seemed like a lifetime ago. Searching for evidence and a possible hidden patron—and maybe killer—lurking somewhere in the Wanderer.

He climbed the steps. "Millie! Are you still up there?"

As Mac reached the left curve of the stairwell, he shined his light on the room at the end of the hall—the figure was still there!

But then he realized what it was: a mannequin. He squinted his eyes; four mannequins actually. Faded, cracked paint detailed their otherwise bare faces, and based on the obvious wear and tear, they were clearly retired from service. Knowing Edith, though, she probably thought she could salvage them and still use them for displays at some point.

A few mannequins stacked to form yet another barrier. This time, the barrier was blocking him from his beloved Millie. But why?

Rage bubbled up in his chest and Mac started hitting the mannequins with his cane. "Move, dammit!" He lost his temper. He gripped the cane hard and swung it over and over at the lifeless body doubles.

They didn't budge.

"Ah!" Mac's chest heaved.

"Mac! Mac! Calm down!" Miguel had stopped about halfway up the stairwell. "It won't work."

"Sorry. Miguel... I'm just so frustrated." Mac turned away from the mannequins.

Miguel walked down the steps. "Let's get back to the others."

As if the other immovable barriers didn't prove it already, this was absolute confirmation that the Wanderer was haunted. It hit Mac much harder now that he couldn't reach Millie. He sucked in a deep breath. He needed to think about what to do next and panicking wasn't helping him put together a plan.

Was the Wanderer itself murdering people? Lady Raftery disappeared into a broom closet. Did the same thing just happen to Millie?

He needed to see if there were more pages in that journal by Wadsworth. That could be his only way to explain the sudden uptick of paranormal activity all over the Wanderer. He needed to speak to Edith about more journals.

Turning back to the hallway, he called, "Millie?! I will be back for you! I promise!"

Mac felt a tremendous sense of despair. A pit formed in his stomach. He didn't quite know how he would figure this one out—he was a former cop. He should be able to have a leg up on whatever was happening here.

More thunder rolled. The rain still pelted the roof; the storm showed no signs of slowing. Mac had two murders to solve, plus a missing fiancé, and an immovable barrier blocking him from the direction of a gunshot that nearly killed a third person.

Mac reached the bottom of the stairs. He had a choice: he could go around to his favorite yellow awning-adorned entrance and brave the powerful storm or wait for it to pass and get help from the GPD. In reality, it wasn't much of a choice at all. It wasn't that far of a walk from the Third Street entrance to the Fulton one. Mac grabbed the door handle.

It didn't turn.

"Aha!" He twisted the knob harder. Nothing.

The door didn't budge.

Mac put his full weight into the door and pushed. When that didn't work, he pulled until his hands throbbed; anything and everything to get out.

Nothing.

The windows.

Mac let go of the knob. He gripped his cane and tried to smash the window. His cane bounced off the glass as if it were plastic shielding.

He wasn't getting through. A sharp tinge of pain traveled through his leg. He overexerted himself by putting too much weight on his leg and swinging his cane wildly like a Southern Congressman in Antebellum America.

He sat on the stairwell and rubbed his leg. He needed to get back to basics. Millie would tell him to relax and think. He needed to get back to old-fashioned detective work and stop searching blindly for clues that weren't there or were blocked off. The pain in his leg lessened but persisted; a perpetual stab that never quite went away.

He had a plan. It was time to learn more about Mr. Forrest and see if Edith knew about any more Wadsworth journals.

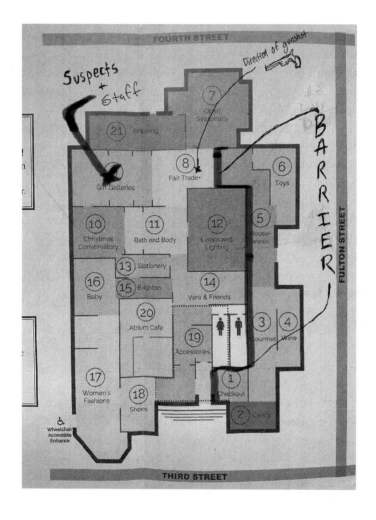

Twenty-Two

Sometimes, Mac thought he could ease his frustration away with sheer will and without actually processing his feelings. He spiked his cane into the wooden floors of the Tiny Wanderer as he made his way back to the fire-lit Gift Galleries. He needed to find answers, Millie, and a killer.

The storm above reflected his mood.

As predicted, the inhabitants of Gift Galleries hadn't moved. Miguel paced the floor and stayed far away from the impenetrable, mysterious barrier. Edith sat next to Rosalie in front of the fireplace; Rose's mascara had dripped in streaks and was now dried in curved, ghostly tracks. The Marlowes kept away from each other, one on each side of the fireplace and on opposite sides of the room. Mr. Forrest still lay unconscious on the floor. Sergeant Yellow, with arms crossed, leaned against the back wall of the room. Robin Billingsley kept staring at her phone as if willing a signal to magically appear. She still seemed oddly cognitively dissonant of the whole situation. Mary Rouge, the disgruntled neighbor, sat cross-legged near the entrance to the Christmas Conservatory, bobbing back and forth.

"Mary. Move," Mac commanded.

"How rude," Mary snapped. "You could say excuse me."

Mac just did his best to maneuver cane-first around her. "No time."

"Any luck finding the shooter?" Edith asked.

"No, Edith. No. We're blocked for some ungodly reason from half of the Wanderer. Now, Mr. Forrest: we need to get his ID, his wallet, and find out everything we can about him. Is he still breathing?" Mac walked over to Forrest and knelt next to him. He grimaced in pain.

"He's still breathing. What gives you the right to take his wallet?" Mary Rouge antagonized.

Mac examined the tourniquet and makeshift bandage Edith had wrapped around his shoulder. Mr. Forrest would live if the storm lifted soon, and they could get an ambulance here... assuming the paramedics could get past the barriers.

Mac patted Forrest's pants pockets and found the bulge of his wallet in his right rear pocket. He flipped open the cloth and Velcro wallet. His driver's license showed a brown-haired, glasses-less, hair perfectly coiffed, Mr. Forrest. He looked strikingly different from his present appearance. Mac also remembered he'd said he was on a road trip visiting various small towns. He had an Illinois license and a Batavia address. The next town to the south.

Mr. Forrest hadn't gotten very far on his road trip.

Something was amiss.

"This is peculiar. Edith, can you confirm this is the same man who was shot and is lying on the floor here unconscious?" Mac walked the wallet with the license displayed over the front to Edith and Rosalie.

Edith nodded then looked to Mr. Forrest. "It's him...just a very different look for him."

"Wait a minute," Rosalie spoke up. "He looks very familiar."

"Really Rose? You recognize him?" Mac kept the wallet in front of her face, lit by the flicker of the fire.

"Yes, I just can't quite remember from where? Gosh, I do recognize this version of him though. He's so familiar."

Mac thumbed through the rest of the wallet. A debit card. A couple of scratch-off lottery tickets. A business card.

"Oh, please Rose. You don't know who the hell he is—you don't remember what day it is half the time!" Mary Rouge barked from her sitting position.

"No, I really do. That isn't nice Mary."

"Shove it, Rose."

Edith broke in, "Hey, watch it, why are you so concerned with Rosalie recognizing him?"

"Yes, why are you so concerned?" Sergeant Yellow came to Rosalie's defense as well.

"She is an idiot. That's why!" Mary Rouge stood up and pointed at Rosalie.

Mac lost it. "Yes, it seems strange that you would attack so viciously, Mary. Maybe you and Mr. Forrest killed Rosalie's friends together as a coordinated plan of attack. Seems odd that you're sitting next to him. Caring for him. You were in the café with Rosalie, Dotty, and Blanche from the start of the storm. You very well could have poisoned the tea Miguel poured them and secured a knife to finish her off when the skylight broke, and the lights went out. Mr. Forrest then followed Dotty into Linens and Lighting and bludgeoned her with a candlestick. Your motive is as simple as you hated them. They owe you money and you're waiting for a chance to get Rosalie next!"

"That is absolute nonsense! I didn't kill those two hags! They are annoying and nauseating neighbors and yes, technically, they do owe me money!" Mary huffed and puffed.

"Mr. O'Malley, you need to back down from your amateur detective act. This storm should clear soon and we can get proper detectives in here to sort this all out." Professor Marlowe spoke up.

"Professor Marlowe, perhaps, *you* hired the suspicious Mr. Forrest to kill your mistress because she was pestering you too much to leave your wife.

Except, Mr. Forrest made a mistake and didn't think his lethal means through. The poison was too weak. Or maybe you didn't hire anyone at all. Maybe you poisoned the tea carafe and did it wrong. You didn't use the proper amount and Blanche was still alive. You had to kill her. Kim was breathing down your neck, so you grabbed a knife and at the opportune moment killed your mistress, Blanche. But Dotty saw or heard you do it in the darkness and commotion. She was next to Blanche the whole time she was unconscious. To cover your tracks, you followed Dotty into Linens and Lighting and killed her too!" Mac's cane flailed as he roared. "The candlestick was a weapon of opportunity!"

"What bullshit! My husband may be an adulterer, but he's not a killer!" Kim Marlowe yelled.

Crack!

A loud crack sounded above him, followed by creaking as if something heavy landed on the roof above and the old wooden trusses struggled under the weight.

"What now?!" Mac yelled.

Twenty-Three

Mac walked toward the weighty cracking above them. It was louder near the front of the building, right about where he thought Millie might be. He hoped she was there. The walk through the darkened halls seemed to help him calm down. He'd spouted accusations like crazy; he never did that. This stormy, volatile, and extremely uncomfortable situation wore on him.

He carried the flashlight toward the sound, walking through the stationary department and up to the bag department. Someone was on the roof above him. *Thud, thud, thud.* They were using a hammer. They were trying to break in!

But...maybe this was a good thing? Maybe it was someone coming to help? Maybe it was Millie trying to escape whatever trap she'd fallen in! The strange happenings in both the lore of the Tiny Wanderer and present-day disturbed Mac deeply. He'd read Wadsworth's journal and right afterward, all hell broke loose.

Coincidence? Mac thought not.

***

Hank worked his flat bar and hammer into the white siding of the Tiny Wanderer. The wand tapped this section on the exterior of the building—this was the spot! His truck hovered just above the rooftop: a spectacular sight if anyone was around to see it, but no one was. The rain still poured down in sheets. Hank was careful not to slip as he pulled away the first plank, hoping to find Millie safe and sound inside.

He jammed the flat bar into another plank of cedar siding and pulled back. Hank did have his hips replaced, but he stood strong on the rooftop; ever determined to help his daughter. He pulled away another plank. And another. He drove the hammer through the plaster walls and, in between the studs, he eventually created a hole as big as a torso.

"Millie!" Hank stuck his head through the hole in the side of the Wanderer. He couldn't see much at all. The darkness of the night sky. The elements working against him. So much rain, so much wind.

"Millie! Are you in there?"

"Dad... is that you?!"

"What are you doing in there? What's going on? I have powers now, I think! I just followed your wand." Hank felt the wand tap his shoulder. He moved aside and Millie's wand flew into the hole.

"I got my wand. Thanks so much, Dad. Fireflies!" Millie used her wand to illuminate her position.

"There you are." Hank investigated the hole he created and then peered inside. He'd revealed a small closet with boxes of hangers in it—and his daughter. Millie looked exhausted, her clothes wrinkled, and her eyes bloodshot.

"I've been stuck in here for like, the past hour. Hang on a sec!" Millie pointed her wand at the closet door. She muttered something and waved it at the door. The door sprang open violently and slammed against the wall.

She was free!

"Well, that did it. What's your next move? Don't you want to get the heck out of the Wanderer?" Hank asked. "Also, how do my truck and I get off the roof?"

"Dad, there have been two murders in here. I'll send you and your truck to the police station to get as much help as possible."

"The streets are flooded like crazy. I've never seen a storm like this in Geneva." Hank pulled away and looked to the deluge and rising water levels of Third.

"Tell Vince and the GPD to trudge through the water, take a boat, emergency rafts, swim, whatever they have to do to get here. Mac and I should have this figured out soon."

"So, I'll just float over to the police station?" Hank asked.

"My magic will get you there safely and park you in the lot."

"Okay, I'll get help."

"Hey Dad."

"Yeah, Mills?"

"Thanks. Love you, Dad."

"I'm just glad you're okay. Be careful. I love you, too. Oh, and Millie—there's no defense for walks." Hank laughed. "Don't let the killer walk."

"Very funny, Dad. Now go get some help!" Millie smiled and then gritted her teeth as she prepped

her wand to send the truck and her Dad to the
GPD station.

Twenty-Four

Millie felt empowered and hopeful now that she and her wand had been reunited. She could also break through whatever barriers the Tiny Wanderer put in her way with the use of her magic. Why on earth the Wanderer would do such things was beyond her. She felt like she would find the answer soon enough. Mac had talked about the possibility of ghosts haunting the old retail mansion and, perhaps, he was right. She didn't actually want him to be right, but something otherworldly could have happened to her. It made sense: she'd lost consciousness and awoke in a small closet bereft of light and hope, let alone any clues as to her the reason for her entrapment.

Millie walked further down the hallway and back to the curved staircase, she'd climbed with Mac just an hour or so before. It felt like ages ago. She noticed a peculiar barricade made of tangled, contorted, mannequins impeding her progress. Heads were at each level and bent legs and arms jutted out in all directions. The light from the tip of her wand also showed the cracked paint and overall garishness of the mannequins. She wasn't sure why the Wanderer had kept them around this long and not scrapped them.

Creepy.

Millie pulled at an elbow joint of the mannequin closest to her. It didn't budge. Much like her previous prison, it was immovable by any physical or natural force. Her supernatural wand would have to move this disaster of a display.

Millie covered her face with her free hand as she pointed her wand at the mannequins. "Repulse!"

As predicted, mannequin body parts flew everywhere. Heads rolled at her feet; a foot bounced off the wall next to her in the narrow hallway. A plastic hand stuck in the ceiling.

Yet it worked.

Her magic moved the barrier.

"Millie! Millie! Is that you?" Mac's voice bellowed from the stairwell.

"Yes!"

"Oh, Thank God."

Millie walked to the stairwell. The sound of Mac's cane driving into the wood floors comforted her. She met him at the curve of the stairwell and embraced her love. She squeezed him hard. He matched the pressure of her squeeze and nearly fell backward on the stairs.

"Whoa!" Mac yelled.

Millie laughed. "I got you."

"I couldn't get through at all. How did you get through the creepy mannequin barrier from hell?" Mac asked.

"Dad brought me my trusty wand!"

"Is that what all the noise was on the roof above? Hank Paderson?!"

"I summoned my wand and he helped me out. He thought he had powers. It was really cute."

"Aww, you know he always wanted powers. Don't tell him he didn't really have them." Mac laughed.

"No, technically, he did have magical powers for a few minutes. The wand did transfer some power to him temporarily," Millie said.

"Well, I'm glad you have your wand back. We'll need it to bust through to the other side. Someone shot Mr. Forrest from the north side of the store. He is still alive, just unconscious. The entire North side of the store is basically blocked off by those impossible barricades. This place IS fricking haunted. I have no idea if Raftery's Ghost is with us or against us. What the hell happened to you?"

"I was locked in a closet. Couldn't get out. I passed out and woke up in darkness in a tiny closet that I couldn't get through. The only thing I could think to do was summon my wand, which of course worked with Dad's help. There're definitely supernatural things happening here. If my magic can move it then it could be another witch or wizard or like you said, or a ghost, maybe."

"After all this and you still aren't convinced Mills?" Mac threw his free hand up.

"Mac, you know we need evidence. Let's investigate the Northside." Millie walked past him and descended the steps; eager to solve the case before Vince and the GPD arrived. Competition did drive her. Playing softball did instill a desire to win.

Twenty-Five

"There's another barrier to the left in The Check-out room. Bust through it and let's do this!" Mac pointed the flashlight toward the barrier.

"Stand back." Millie pointed her wand.

"I know the drill."

"Repulse!" Millie commanded magic with ease, strength, and a cunning, seasoned resolve. The makeshift barrier of chairs and tables crumbled and gave way.

"We must be careful heading in there. We were trapped in here. I can't even open the front door or a window; only you can with that wand. And the shooter is somewhere on this side of the Wanderer with a live gun. He or she fired two shots at Mr. Forrest." Mac stood beside Millie at the newfound entrance to the Northside of the Wanderer.

"I can cast a spell that illuminates the whole area. We'll find the shooter quickly."

"Oh yeah, like you did in that guy's garage that one time. The fireflies one. I remember."

"Yes, *sometimes* you do impress me. You aren't as dumb as you look." Millie smiled.

"Ha! Am I glad you're back? Not really sure at the moment." Mac laughed. Their banter was one of the things he loved most about their relationship.

"Fireflies!" Millie waved her wand and sparks of light shot out, filling the room. She kept the rotation of her wand constant as more and more sparks emerged and raced to extinguish the darkness.

"Let's go, Mac." Millie kept her wand moving as she slowly walked into the Northside of the

Wanderer. Cash registers to the left and the candy section just down a couple stairs to the right.

Mac followed. He was happy to have Millie back by his side. Usually, things improved with her around. Yes, people seemed to die around them frequently, but still: their union felt right. She was one thing he could count on during a night where nothing went favorably or to his advantage in any way, shape, or form. He could count on the love of his life to be there.

The conundrum-cracking couple would find the solution.

The pair followed the small orbs of light that hugged the ceiling and found themselves in a room filled with bags of goodies, treats, and delectable treats. Bags of chocolates assorted colorful candies and the smell of sugar comforted Mac.

"Clear. Edith wouldn't mind if we just pigged out in here, right? I'm super hungry." Millie took a deep breath.

"I know I'm super hungry, too. So much for dinner with Hank and Beck. I love the Candy Room, though!" Mac picked up a Tiny Wanderer-labeled bag with a picture of the great mansion, the legacy brand of Geneva.

Millie followed the magical trail of dancing lights into the kitchen and cooking wares area, the Gourmet section of the Wanderer. To the right of Gourmet, a doorless threshold split off another room. The Wine section.

"I'll split off to the right. Millie, you head straight."

"Don't tell me what to do." Millie balked but listened.

"Whatevs. I'll check out the wine section." Mac followed Millie into Gourmet and then turned right into the Wine section. He still used the flashlight; he swept the beam slowly examining the wine racks and coffee-table books on display in the area. The wooden racks lined the walls and reached to the end of the room, about twenty feet away and to another door. The door's paint looked stripped, with cracks and holes not unlike Nicholson's work in an early 80s horror flick. It looked like someone tried to get out this way but couldn't—not unlike Mac earlier.

He walked closer to the damaged but shut, door.

"Don't come any..." a deep voice sounded from the corner of the room.

Even with Millie's magic light above, Mac couldn't place exactly where the voice came from. It sounded like it was near the door, but not quite next to it. He shined his torch to the corners and the ground.

And he saw a figure: someone was sitting on the floor. A man. An empty bottle of red wine was in his left hand and the gun that shot Mr. Forrest in the other.

"Trapped. Trappety Trappety. Can't find a way outta this horrible place. Now there's lights outta nowhere lights and a—who are you?!" The man rambled.

Mac shined the torch in the man's eyes. "Drop the weapon."

The man's face was angular as if it was chiseled from hard stone. His chin was covered in gray stubble; he had a bald head and bags under his eyes. Physically, he looked to be in good shape, likely from years of disciplined exercise. At the moment, though, he was inebriated. The gunman apparently chose to wallow in the bottle instead of continuing to find a way out.

"A cop! Great! A cop. Wonderful. Wait minute.... if you got in here, maybe you can help me get out. Help me! Help me the get the hell outta here!" The drunken gunman pointed the pistol at Mac.

Twenty-Six

"We can find a way out of this together. And I'm not a cop. I'm just a man stuck in here like you. I was searching the rooms for others," Mac said. "Once the storm clears, we'll get out of here."

The man continued rambling. "How did your ass get in here? I was blocked from the other side of this old dump. And blocked from getting out! This place is haunted. We are doomed to Hell. How do I know you're real and not some ghost or demon or some shit?"

Mac hoped Millie heard all of this. She had to...right?

"I found a way through. I know stuff was stacked up so we couldn't get past easily. I just crawled through a hole. Why don't you come with me? There are others in here and we can all find a way out together. But that gun. You need to drop the gun."

"See, that's why I think you're a damn cop. The way you say things. Your tone. I've been around cops before. Most I paid off. You *are* a damn cop!" The gunman fired at Mac.

The muffled *pew* of the hitman's silenced weapon struck fear in Mac's heart. A bottle of wine burst into shattered glass next to him. Red; it could be confused with blood sprayed on his face.

Mac ducked. A sharp pain raced through his injured leg. He crawled as fast as he could toward the drunken gunman. His cane was in one hand and the still-lit flashlight in the other.

Suddenly, the Fireflies that dotted the ceiling vanished, leaving Mac's torch the only source of light.

The sound of another shot slammed into the ground in front of Mac. He rolled to the left and hit the wall. Some bottles rattled and one fell behind him. As the glass bottle shattered, Mac quickly turned off the flashlight.

The consistent lack of light that dominated the evening provided cover for Mac. He continued his crawl toward the gun-wielding drunk.

"Where did the creepy ghost lights go?!"

Mac's ears pinpointed the hitman's locale.

He crawled closer and closer, his heart beat faster and faster. He stayed low in the hope that the idiot would keep firing above him. He would have had him already if it weren't for his leg injury.

A bright laser beam shot forth from the left end of the room. An emerald green, serpentine, line of light. A crackling rope of energy squeezed the suspect and yanked him from the ground. He dropped the gun and the bottle of wine.

Millie walked in and held out her wand: the source of the green rope tied around Mac's newest adversary. She flicked her wand up and the rope raised the bad guy against the wine rack. His head touched the ceiling.

"Nice, Mills!" Mac performed a push-up and rose to his knees.

"I should be able to hold him for a few minutes, but we should get something to tie him up with."

"Why did you shoot Forrest?" Mac leaned on his cane and looked up at the restrained man. He patted the drunk's pockets and found his wallet.

"Frank Konidaris. Okay Frank, spit it out. Or don't and worse things will happen to you."

"Nice looking gal there, boss. She yours? Saw her upstairs earlier. Sweet piece of ass there." Frank laughed.

"Millie, can you squeeze him harder?"

"At will." Millie grimaced and the slithering rope tightened around the elevated Frank.

"Oh shit...All right. All right! Forrest. Forrest. You mean Carroll, Freddie Carroll. I was here to shoot that lanky moron. He owes me money. And he had until yesterday to pay up. Jesus, can you ease up? I think I'm gonna puke."

"Describe Freddie."

"The lanky idiot dyed his hair blond and wore glasses and that scraggly beard thinking he could fool me. I've been watchin' him for the past week. Followed him here. Figured with the power out and the storm, I could shoot him and get the hell outta here."

"How did you get in here? And when?" Mac asked.

"During the storm, I walked in the front door and then hid upstairs when I heard you two comin'. I hid in one of the rooms and saw this chick get pulled into a closet by some ungodly force. I panicked and found another stairway. A butler's stair-case, I guess ya call it, and came down and decided I needed to speed things up. So, I shot at Freddie."

"You shot twice. One bullet hit him in the shoul-der. Your other shot missed the mark. Why? Are you just that bad of a shot?"

"That's when things got weirder. Something made me miss my shot."

"What something?"

"Probably the same shit that moved you into that closet! My god this is so tight..." Frank stared at Millie.

"Tell us more about Forrest, I mean, Freddie. We need to know more." Mac pressed.

"A degenerate gambler. He owes a lot of money. Bets on everything. Simple. This is routine work for me. I'm gonna puke. Seriously, ease up lady!"

"Mac, let's tie him up. This is getting old." Millie rubbed her wand-wielding arm.

Mac pulled handcuffs from his jacket. "I got it."

"You still carry cuffs with you?" Millie asked.

"Yes, so what?" Mac laughed. "Okay, let him go. I got him."

Millie let the green energy rope dissipate and Frank fell to the ground.

Mac turned on his flashlight and walked over to him. The smell of alcohol assaulted his nose. Frank hit the bottles of wine hard—real hard. Mac held his breath and quickly handcuffed him to the wine rack. He didn't want to have to find him in the many, many rooms of the Wanderer should he attempt an escape.

"I knew you were a cop...dirty cop. She like a witch or something? What the hell is going on in this place? Am I in hell?!" Frank gave Mac the finger with his free hand.

"Yeah, yeah, yeah. Keep talking Frank. You already confessed to attempted murder." Mac shook his head.

Millie's magical sparks of light populated the Wine Room once more.

"Mac, we should really get back to the others," Millie said.

"Just a second, Frank, you said you followed Forrest, sorry Freddie, for a while. What car does he drive?"

"I ain't helping you anymore." Frank shook his head then burped.

"Millie, have any curses for Frank?"

"He drives a broken-down old Lexus. It is outside parked near that yellow awning."

"Thanks Frank. We'll get you to jail soon, I promise." Mac patted Frank's head.

"Anywhere is better than here."

Mac and Millie walked into the Gourmet section and away from Frank.

"Should we be worried that Frank knows I'm a witch?"

"Frank is very drunk and there are plenty of other things neither he nor we can explain going on in here tonight. I think I may have figured out who murdered Dotty and Blanche." Mac fished the patron formerly known as Mr. Forrest's wallet out of his pocket.

"How do you know? I mean it's probably Frank, right?" Millie asked.

"Here it is. The business card. I never really looked at it."　Mac examined the faded business card.

"Why is that important?" Millie asked.

"Frederick Carroll, Chaparo Insurance Services. Your wand can get us out of here, right? We have to search his car."

Twenty-Seven

After a thorough search of the broken-down old
Lexus, Millie made short work of the barrier in
Fair Trade and dismantled it with magic. Mac
and Millie walked into the Gift Galleries section
of the Tiny Wanderer. The rainfall pelting the
roof had softened to a smattering of drops from
the consistent pall of the storm. Mac called roll
in his head: Rosalie, Yellow, Rouge, Robin, the
Marlowes, Forrest, Edith, and Miguel were around
the fireplace. All of them were accounted for. They
were all in various states of consciousness. Some
were sprawled out on the floor sleeping. Profes-

sor Marlowe paced the floor. Sergeant Yellow did pushups and then got up and performed high knees. Mr. Forrest—or Fred—still lay unconscious on the floor.

"Mac! Millie! You're back!" Edith and Miguel shouted.

"The storm's letting up. Can we get out of here?" Sergeant Yellow bellowed.

Mary Rouge barked, "I think it's safe for us to go. Now! Let us out."

The lights flickered for a second.

"Oh goodie, power might come back on!" Edith exclaimed.

"Rose, you said you thought Mr. Forrest looked familiar?" Mac asked.

Rosalie didn't look good. Grief had taken a hefty toll on her. Her best friends had died this night; the people she spent every day with. She leaned heavily against the wall by the fireplace. "Yes, he does look familiar. I still can't place him, though."

"Perhaps this will help you remember." Mac stepped over Forrest and to Rose. He showed her the card.

"What does it say? I don't have my readers."

"It says Frederick Carrol of Chaparo Insurance. That ring any bells?"

"Oh my. Oh my. Yes! Yes, it does."

"Oh please!" Mary Rouge shouted.

"Mary! Shut it!" Millie yelled.

"Does Mr. Forrest look like Mr. Carroll to you, Rose? Did Mr. Carroll have brown hair? Come with me, Rose." Mac walked her to Forrest's side. He pushed and parted the gunshot wound victim's hair.

"He has brown roots all right. So what?" Professor Marlowe rumbled.

"Rose, have you or your friends worked with Chaparo Insurance Services?"

"Not worked per se, but Mr. Carroll came to one of our church's lunch events. He presented about life insurance and long-term care options. We all bought a policy from him. Mr. Forrest does look an awful lot like Mr. Carroll. The nice man we bought our policies from!"

"Rose, you said our policies. Whose policies exactly?"

"Yes, we all bought $250,000 policies from him. Dotty, Blanche, and I."

"Did you do all of this electronically or was everything done with paper, Rose?"

"All on paper. We didn't use any computers or anything."

"Who did you all set as the beneficiary for these policies? According to documents found in Mr. Forrest's car, you all made Mr. Carroll the beneficiary."

"That isn't true! We made our kids the beneficiaries."

"Mr. Forrest, formerly Mr. Carroll the insurance agent, murdered your friends, Rose. He tried to poison you by dropping arsenic into the tea. But he didn't put in enough to make it lethal. Blanche had a strong reaction to it but didn't die. Had she ingested more, it might have done the trick. And in the perfect storm of the skylight cracking and the power outage, Frederick found a knife in the café and used it to finish off Blanche. He dropped the knife and then proceeded to follow Dotty into Linens and Lighting, where he very quickly grabbed a candlestick off one of the displays and hit her over the head with it. Then, he moved her body behind the counter. In an effort to deflect suspicion and blame, he made me aware of Dotty's dead body. He also offered help immediately, earnestly, as if he had something to hide. His bravery and calmness under pressure seemed odd to me, considering the circumstances. Most people would be rattled, but he came off a bit too forced."

Marlowe shook his head. "How did he do all of that so quickly and in the dark?"

"He's a capable thirty-three-year-old male. He has the physical prowess and a cellphone, therefore a flashlight, to help guide him in the dark. He took advantage of the situation and moved quickly. Go ahead, Marlowe, examine him for a cellphone and you'll probably find a pair of gloves in his jacket or in his back pocket."

"Why wouldn't he try to escape and just take the 500k?" Mary Rouge asked. "Also, that doesn't explain who shot him."

Professor Marlowe patted down Frederick Carroll and found both a cellphone and gloves. "Mac is right. Cellphone with power, but no signal, and gloves. I better drop the gloves."

"So glad you asked Mary. In the Wine Room, you will find a Mr. Frank Konidaris. He already confessed to the attempted murder of Mr. Forrest aka Mr. Carroll. Fred owes Frank a lot of money. Gambling money. Bad bets. Debts that needed paying. Although clearly, Mr. Carroll had no intention of paying Frank and spent a considerable amount of time changing identities and going to great lengths to avoid him."

The lights flickered for a few seconds, and then turned on.

Power restored.

Mac pointed his cane to another suspect, "Robin Billingsley, newest staff member of the Wanderer. You said you were with Mr. Forrest in the café and stayed with each other in the commotion after the Atrium Café's skylight and roof collapsed. You said you discovered the body together, correct?"

"It was dark. Oh no, please. I am not part of this. He was sitting closer to the café exit. I swear. He made it into Linens and Lighting first. Please. I was in shock when you asked me earlier. I had nothing to do with this. Please. I was looking for my purse as I said when I heard Mr. Forrest yell about the body. I was close as I was in the same room at the same time and walked over and stared at the body in shock. Please." Robin's previous cold and distant demeanor changed. Tears streamed down her face. Her chest heaved.

Either she was a great actress or genuine. Mac felt as though she told the truth.

"Edith, can you vouch for her?" Mac looked to Edith.

"I personally hired her Mac. She is telling the truth. I moved her assignment into toys mid-shift today from Linens and Lighting, which is why her purse was behind the Linens counter."

Frederick Carroll rose from the ground and shoved Professor Marlowe down. He grabbed his shoulder. The murderer ran through Fair Trade in the direction Frank shot him from and turned right toward Housewares—and the side door with the yellow awning.

"Millie! Stop him!" Mac yelled.

Millie hated to run but felt confident in her sprinting ability to overtake Fred in a matter of

seconds. Many base-running drills over a long pe-
riod of her youth built up her leg muscles. Thank
you Hank!

Fred hit some dishes on his way to the door. The
stacks crashed and shattered, launching shards
into the air. Millie's long legs easily carried her
over the mess—like leaping over the Short Stop!
—and she continued her pursuit.

She was only a couple of feet away from him. She
didn't want to use her magic. She extended her
right arm to grab him.

Fred turned for the door. He gripped the handle
and Millie saw him slip, hit the floor, and then crawl
backward on his elbows.

"Millie!" Hank Paderson's voice bellowed from
the doorway.

"Dad! He's the killer! Be careful!

"Oh, don't worry! I did what you said to do!"
Hank yelled.

Millie reached the doorway and the scrambling Fred Carroll. She watched as four officers of the Geneva Police Department poured in and captured Fred Carroll. Hank walked in behind them.

"Thanks Dad."

Hank Paderson smiled at his daughter. His face turned serious and he whispered, "I think my powers are gone."

"Aww, Dad." Millie hugged her father.

"Your mother will never believe me."

"She won't."

Hank and Millie laughed.

Twenty-Eight

TWO WEEKS LATER

Millie and Mac shopped the Tiny Wanderer and added items to their wedding shower registry. They looked for pots and pans in Housewares and then made their way into Linens and Lighting.

Mac looked over to the counter where Dotty was murdered. He huffed. "I suppose we are just going to have to be okay with not really knowing why you were shoved in a closet. And parts of the Wanderer were blocked off by impenetrable barriers and we couldn't get out."

"Wrong. My magic did bust through the barriers." Millie picked up a blanket and examined it.

"Yes, but who or what created the barriers in the first place?" Mac was sure to keep his voice down as to not startle any other customers. The Tiny Wanderer had just reopened after the monumental storm.

"We've been over this again and again for two weeks, Mac. Sometimes, things just can't be solved or fixed or whatever. In a way, I'm glad I was put into that closet. Frank the mobster was upstairs with me. Remember?" Millie put the blanket down.

"So, you think this place is haunted by benevolent hero ghosts or something?"

"I don't know about that. But the Wanderer did aid us in our investigation. It kept Frank trapped."

"Yes, but if it was helping me, why not let me in and let me get out?"

"My magic was able to do that. I don't know, again, Mac, some things just can't be explained and fit into a nice, proper box."

"Though, you do agree now that this place is haunted. Lady Raftery could still be here haunting the Wanderer."

Millie sighed. "Yes, there is a strong possibility that this place is haunted. I will give you that."

"Hey, you two, keep that talk down!" Edit tapped on Mac's back. "Mac here. I found another diary."

"What? Really?"

Millie shook her head. "Go ahead and read it. I want to keep shopping."

"It'll only take a few minutes! Thanks Edith!" Mac walked into the café. The atrium portion was still being fixed and the skylight replacement was to be in next week.

He sat at a table above the Atrium area and opened the diary.

"*I returned to the very same broom closet and shook my head in disbelief. Turns out, a young woman didn't enter a broom closet. There was another door beyond that served as a powder room. My mistake. She fit the description of the noble daughter. One Lady Raftery, I had found her at last. It was perhaps the most critical moment of my life's journey. It was the turning point of the case and one that would be the most incredible moment of my life. Lady Raftery was the most beautiful sight I'd ever seen. A presence I hadn't felt before in my thirty years. It gave me a feeling of peace combined with a happiness so satisfactory. I felt connected to her. I informed her parents of her whereabouts and safety. We met in the Tiny Wanderer and within weeks, we fell deeply in love. The Tiny Wanderer quickly became our favorite spot. Lady Raftery helped form a tea-time tradition in this beautiful mansion. She*

had no intentions of leaving America and wanted
to stay in Geneva. As it turns out, I had the same
intention.

Lady Raftery and I walked the river and felt
as if Geneva was our home. We made it so. Lady
Raftery and I married and invested in the Tiny
Wanderer, becoming part owners of the great
retail mansion. We wanted to preserve the place
we'd met and fell in love. With a firm financial
investment, we swore to protect The Tiny Wanderer for the foreseeable future.

We sit here together and have made good on
our promise to keep the Tiny Wanderer a Geneva destination. One of the great joys of our lives
has been in the traditions formed in our adopted
home, the Christmas events, summer festivals,
and of course the people and families who frequent our favourite place so often. They come
back repeatedly to walk the many rooms, have
a spot of tea, shop, and just be here. The length

of their patronage now spans generations. I still find that hard to believe.

We shall always be here to champion this special place even long after we are gone. Lady Raftery and I will always be here in spirit."
-Wadsworth of Third Street (formerly Baker Street)

THE END

The Mac and Millie Mystery Series!

More Geneva! More Fun! More Magic!

JB MICHAELS

About Author

JB Michaels is a USA Today Bestselling Author and Amazon Bestselling Author. His work has won 7 Literary Achievement Awards over the span of his career starting with the wondrous and imaginative Tannenbaum Tailors series to the dark and thrilling Chronicles of the Order series. JB's books have been read around the world, reached #1 in multiple categories, and continue to delight readers both young and old alike. Head to mistermichaels.com to learn more!